jE HIGUERA Donna
El Cucuy is scared, too! /
Higuera, Donna Barba,

WITHDRAWN
SEP 2 2 2021

D0467903

*Pronounced *el ku-koo-ee*

For my Elena.
You've traveled so far, Little One.
¡Eres la más fuerte y valiente!
—D. H.

For Pipe.
Thank you for the scary nights
and the secret toy parties that
made everything better.
—J. P.

The illustrations in this book were made digitally on a tablet that was carried around everywhere.

Cataloging-in-Publication Data has been applied for and may be obtained from the Library of Congress.

ISBN 978-1-4197-4445-7

Text copyright © 2021 Donna Barba Higuera
Illustrations copyright © 2021 Juliana Perdomo
Book design by Heather Kelly

Published in 2021 by Abrams Books for Young Readers, an imprint of ABRAMS. All rights reserved. No portion of this book may be reproduced, stored in a retrieval system, or transmitted in any form or by any means, mechanical, electronic, photocopying, recording, or otherwise, whout written permission from the publisher.

Printed and bound in China
10 9 8 7 6 5 4 3 2 1

Abrams Books for Young Readers are available at special discounts when purchased in quantity for premiums and promotions as well as fundraising or educational use. Special editions can also be created to specification. For details, contact specialsales@abramsbooks.com or the address below.

Abrams® is a registered trademark of Harry N. Abrams, Inc.

ABRAMS The Art of Books
195 Broadway, New York, NY 10007
abramsbooks.com

EL CUCUY IS SCARED, TOO!

STORY BY
DONNA BARBA
HIGUERA

PICTURES BY
JULIANA
PERDOMO

Abrams Books for Young Readers
New York

Ramón can't sleep.

El Cucuy can't sleep either.

¡BUUUM!

"You are not scared of me?
You were always terrified
of me before."

"Other things are scarier to me now."

El Cucuy sighs. "Yo también."

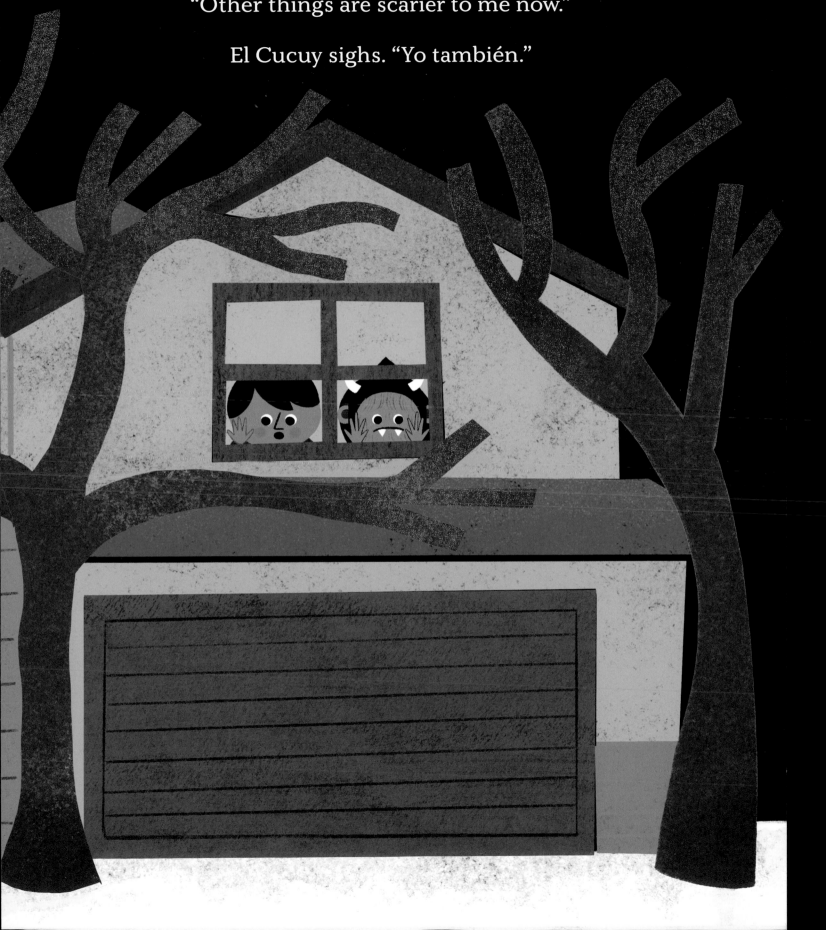

"I miss our old casita," Ramón says.

"Yo también." El Cucuy's shoulders sag. "I miss our old home, too.
I miss the desert wind and the coyotes singing."

"¡Dios mio!
What is that?"

Uuuuuuuu
Uuuu Uuuuu

"Está bien," Ramón reassures El Cucuy. "It is only the new sounds of where we live now. We will get used to it."

"But," Ramón worries, "this new school is much bigger.
What if the library doesn't have a quiet corner where I can read?"

"You are right. Everything here is larger and lighter.
There are so few small, dark places where I can hide."

"Don't be nervous. You will learn where things are.
If you are scared, I can ask a teacher or librarian
where there is a safe place for you to go."

"But now I am thinking . . . the kids at my new school
might not be like my old friends," Ramón says. "What if my clothes
are not like theirs? What if they make fun of the way I speak?
Maybe I should not talk at all."

El Cucuy sighs. "I don't have any amigos here either.
I don't feel like growling or howling.
No one will even know to be afraid of me."

Ramón pats El Cucuy on the shoulder. "Eres fuerte . . . and brave. You will make new friends. They might even be afraid of you. You will have to show them you are strong and valiente."

"Think of all the times I knew you'd crawled under my bed, just waiting to frighten me," Ramón says, to cheer El Cucuy up.

"You were brave, too. You jumped up and down
on the bed, so I ran back to my pot!"

"Yes. And do you remember the time you howled outside
and scratched on my window to keep me awake? ¡Ay, qué miedo!"

El Cucuy smiles. "And you didn't even listen. You sang 'Cielito Lindo' to drown out my screeches until you fell asleep."

Ramón nudges El Cucuy. "Or the time you made your eyes
glow from inside the closet? ¡Qué horror!"

"And you grabbed a flashlight and shined it right at me,
so I had to hide my eyes."

"You really think I am strong and brave?" El Cucuy asks.

Ramón grins.

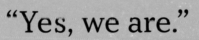
"Yes, we are."

AUTHOR'S NOTE

El Cucuy, also known as the Mexican Boogeyman, strikes terror in children. El Cucuy sometimes goes by El Cuco or El Chamuco, depending on the region of the Southwestern United States or Mexico. But he lives in many South American countries and takes on different forms. In Brazil, *she* is known by A Cuca.

Generations of Latin American mothers and grandmothers have used El Cucuy as a tool to get children to behave. Most families have an El Cucuy. My El Cucuy lived in my abuela's closet (although he often hid behind a large cactus). I never actually saw him, but he WAS THERE.

ILLUSTRATOR'S NOTE

I grew up in a culture where magical realism was at the core of our lives. This is why many fantastic and scary creatures were often mentioned. These creatures are a mixture of wild animals, nature, and lost souls that wander the corners of each Colombian region. My older cousin Pipe used to scare me with these tales. I remember he sometimes mentioned El Coco, a monster who would come after kids if they didn't behave; but after his detailed descriptions, I would still have a wonderful sleep. He, on the other hand, would stay wide awake.